A City Christmas Tree

Rebecca Bond

Megan Tingley Books

LITTLE, BROWN AND COMPANY

New York ⬥ Boston

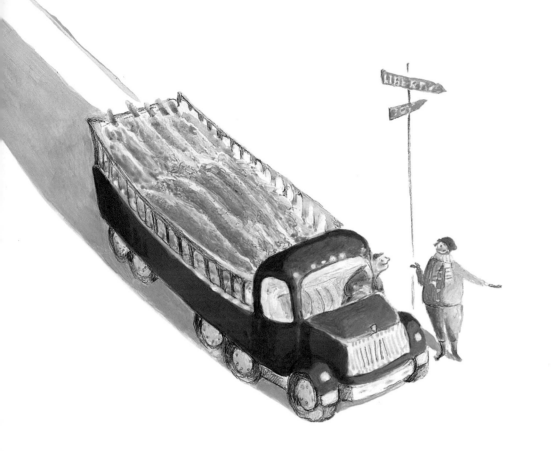

For Papa,
who loved Christmas most

Also by Rebecca Bond:
Just Like a Baby
Bravo, Maurice!
When Marcus Moore Moved In

Little, Brown and Company

Time Warner Book Group
1271 Avenue of the Americas, New York, NY 10020
Visit our Web site at www.lb-kids.com

First Edition: October 2005

Library of Congress Cataloging-in-Publication Data

Bond, Rebecca, 1972-
A city Christmas tree / Rebecca Bond.—1st ed.
p. cm.
Summary: Maggie visits the Christmas tree man on Liberty Street,
then brings her brothers, sister, and finally her parents, as they each dream
their own dreams of what it means to have a Christmas tree in the city.
ISBN 0-316-53731-4
[1. Christmas trees—Fiction. 2. Christmas—Fiction.] I. Title.

PZ7.B63686Ci 2005
[E]—dc22   2004028893

10 9 8 7 6 5 4 3 2 1

TWP

Printed in Singapore

The illustrations for this book were done in acrylic.

When the Christmas tree man set up his shop
on Liberty Street at the end of the block,
it started the city all dreaming great dreams
of a city Christmas tree.

Maggie Laroche was the first to come,
just Maggie alone on Monday day.
She twirled herself to a standstill stop
by a tree at the end of the block.

"Isn't it fine?" asked the tree man, excited.
"Oh yes!" breathed Maggie. "It is! It is!"

And she leaned in close, and she dreamed her dreams
of a city Christmas tree.

For the smell of city Christmas trees
to Maggie Laroche was wild and windy.
It spiced up the air with the freshest of zest,
like a day in the spray of the sea.

Maggie Laroche came back with her brother Teddy
together on Tuesday day.
They twirled and skipped down Liberty Street
to the tree at the end of the block.

"Isn't it fine?" asked Maggie, excited.
"Oh yes!" sighed Teddy. "It is! It is!"

And he looked and he laughed and he dreamed his dreams
of a city Christmas tree.

For to Teddy Laroche it was the color,
the deeply, densely green-blue hue.

He felt he was home in the heart of the woods,
all brightly and lushly alive.

Maggie and Teddy came back with their brother, Lucas,
together on Wednesday day.
They twirled and skipped and bounced down the street
to the tree at the end of the block.

"Isn't it fine?" asked Teddy, excited.

"Oh yes!" beamed Lucas. "It is! It is!"

And he closed his eyes and he dreamed his dreams
of a city Christmas tree.

For to Lucas Laroche it was the tree lights.
They warmed up the feelings inside of his chest.

They dazzled and glittered like lantern-lit globes.
Together they shimmered like stars.

Maggie and Teddy and Lucas came back
with their sister, Ellie, on Thursday day.
They twirled and skipped and bounced and danced
to the tree at the end of the block.

"Isn't it fine?" asked Lucas, excited.

"Oh yes!" whispered Ellie. "It is! It is!"

And she cooed and she crooned and she dreamed her dreams of a city Christmas tree.

To Ellie Laroche it was the angel,
with her marvelous wings and her butterfly grace.
She would keep careful watch on the world just below,
from her spot at the top of the tree.

Maggie and Teddy and Lucas and Ellie
came back with their parents on Friday day.
They twirled and skipped and bounced and danced,
and like a small parade, they pranced
all the way down Liberty Street
to the tree at the end of the block.

"Isn't it fine?" asked Ellie, excited.
"Oh yes!" sang her parents. "It is! It is!"

And they smiled their smiles
and dreamed their dreams
of a city Christmas tree.

And to Mother and Father, it was the family,
who would come from far places with boxes and bags,
crossing the landscapes, the seascapes, the skies,
to share all together this tree.

And so that day they took their tree.
They carried it high on Liberty Street.
They carried it tightly but tenderly, too.

They carried it merrily home.

And Saturday day—Finally! At last!
Their tree went up as snow came down.

And the family turned like tops all around it.
They talked and they laughed
and they danced and they glowed!

For they were just happy—high up in their dreams of a city Christmas tree.

And when Sunday came in as quiet as quiet,
and the world was perfect and it was dark,

there were only the lights all bright in the city
of hundreds of Christmas-tree trees.